Tom and the
Dark Knight

Creaky Castle

Tom and the Dark Knight

Tony Bradman

Illustrated by

Stephen Parkhouse

USBORNE

For Alfie and Ruby!

First published in the UK in 2008 by Usborne Publishing Ltd., Usborne House, 83-85 Saffron Hill, London EC1N 8RT, England. www.usborne.com

Text copyright © Tony Bradman, 2008
Illustration copyright © Usborne Publishing Ltd., 2008

A CIP catalogue record for this book is available from the British Library.

FMAMJJASOND/08
ISBN 9780746072288
Printed in Great Britain.

Contents

Cast of Characters

Thomas Bailey
Our hero!

Matilda Bailey
Thomas's scary sister

Lady Eleanor Bailey
Thomas's even scarier mum

Sir John Bailey
Thomas's dad

Sparky
Thomas's pet dragon

Mouldy
One of Sir John Bailey's
men-at-arms

Mott
The family dog

Harry Fitzhooley
The Dark Knight's
boastful son

Sir Richard Fitzhooley
AKA the Dark Knight

Faldor
A mad wizard

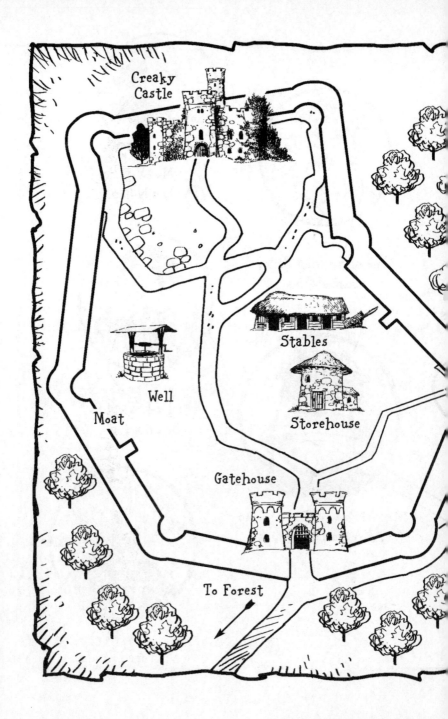

Creaky
Castle

Stables

Well

Storehouse

Moat

Gatehouse

To Forest

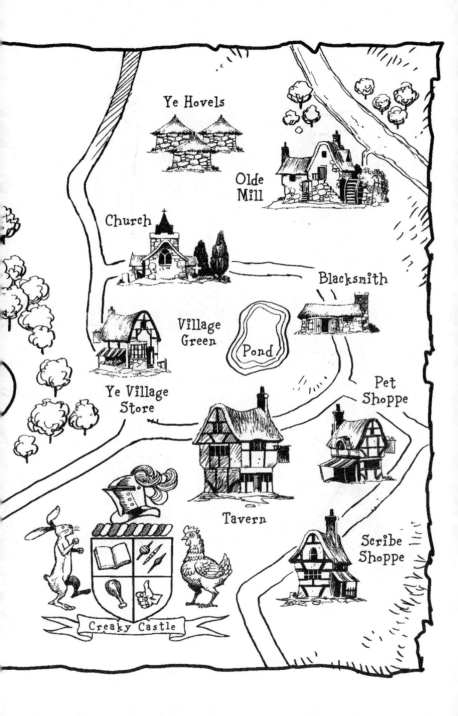

Ye Hovels

Olde Mill

Church

Blacksmith

Village Green

Pond

Ye Village Store

Pet Shoppe

Tavern

Scribe Shoppe

Creaky Castle

Chapter One

A Dream Come True

Thomas Bailey peeked out from behind an old cart in the courtyard of his home, Creaky Castle. A couple of men-at-arms were leaning on their pikes by the main gate, but no one else was in sight. There certainly wasn't any sign of his mother, Lady Eleanor, and Thomas smiled.

He was feeling pretty pleased with himself. He had managed to keep out of Mother's way all morning, which meant he hadn't been given any boring chores to do, so he had been able to focus entirely on having fun.

"Come on, Sparky," he whispered, continuing
to scan the courtyard. "We'll slip out and go down
to the woods. You can roast some chestnuts if you
like, although you'll have to make sure you don't
get overexcited and set fire to any trees this time,
okay? Hey, did you hear me, Sparky?"

Thomas glanced over his shoulder...and his blood
ran cold. He had expected his enormous pet dragon
to be sitting right behind him, but Sparky was
nowhere to be seen. Mother was standing there

instead, staring at him and seeming none too pleased at what she'd just heard.

"Well, I suppose that solves the mystery of last week's forest fire," she said, one stern eyebrow raised. "Of course, I should have guessed you and your dragon had something to do with it. That beast has been nothing but trouble ever since you bought him. Still, you've given me a good idea..."

"Have I?" asked Thomas, a feeling of confusion beginning to creep over him. Mother was behaving very strangely. She should be shouting at him by now, but her cross expression had suddenly vanished. She was gazing at a corner of the courtyard, looking thoughtful and nodding to herself.

"Umm, yes, that might work..." she murmured at last. Then she turned back to her son. "Anyway, don't just stand there looking dozy, Thomas," she said. "Your father and sister are waiting for us in the Great Hall. We could have got started ages ago if it hadn't taken me so long to find you."

13

She marched off, heading for the Keep, and Thomas scurried after her. "Get started on what?" he said, intrigued, but Mother didn't answer.

Suddenly Sparky appeared from behind the stables. The dragon trailed closely behind Thomas, giving off a plaintive noise, a sort of sad mooing.

"Huh, it's no good being all pathetic and sorry now, is it?" Thomas hissed. "You could at least have given me some kind of warning."

"He wouldn't have dared," said Lady Eleanor, striding into the Keep.

Thomas followed, Sparky squeezed through behind him, and soon the

three of them arrived in the Great Hall. Sir John and Matilda were sitting together on one side of the long dining table. On the table itself were several thick rolls of parchment, a big ink pot and a large quill pen.

Sparky tiptoed quietly over to lie beside Mott, the family's ancient wolfhound. Mott growled, and moved off to sit under the table near Sir John. Sparky rested his huge head on his paws, puffs of white smoke emerging every now and again from his nostrils.

"Ah, Tom, so your mother finally tracked you down," said Sir John, stroking Mott. "Sit over here and tell me what you've been up to."

"Actually, I'd rather we just got on with it," muttered Matilda. "*Some* of us might have better things to do than to hang around in here all day."

"Er...get on with *what,* exactly?" asked Thomas, taking the seat next to his father. "I wish somebody would just tell me what's going on."

"Apparently Mother has an announcement to make," said Matilda.

"That's quite correct, Matilda," said Lady Eleanor in her special serious voice. "Now sit up and pay attention, please. What I have to say is rather important. I'm afraid that yet again we've got money problems, but—"

"So what's new?" said Matilda. "We're always short of money."

"Oh no, hardly *always*, Matilda," grumbled Sir John. "Just, well...most of the time. Anyway, money isn't the most important thing in life, is it?

And although it would be lovely to have a little more, we *do* seem to get by."

"Personally speaking, I've had more than enough of *getting by*," said Lady Eleanor. "So I've been doing some thinking, and I believe I've come up with a way for us to make money. A *lot* of money, perhaps."

"Why, that's wonderful, dear," said Sir John, beaming at his wife. "I wish I was as brilliant as you. Er...what exactly did you have in mind?"

"I'm going to put on a Grand Jousting Tournament," said Lady Eleanor. "We can invite lots of knights, charge each one an entry fee, and—"

"A Grand Jousting Tournament?" squeaked Thomas, utterly amazed. He could hardly believe his ears. "What, right here in...Creaky Castle?"

It was a dream come true. Thomas was obsessed with tournaments. He had a subscription to *CLAAAAANG!*, the jousting magazine, and a full set of *Top Thumps*, the cards featuring pictures of jousters and statistics of their competition performances. But he had never been to a tournament, not once, and he had almost given up hope of going to one. He could hardly believe that a tournament was about to come to him instead.

"Yes, Thomas," sighed Mother. "As I was saying, I want to—"

"Whoa, how cool is that?" said Matilda, grinning at her brother. Thomas knew she was obsessed with tournaments too. In fact, she liked nothing better than to wear armour, and she was pretty handy with a lance herself. "*I* won't have to pay an entry fee, will I?" she added.

"Certainly not," snapped Mother. "Because you won't be—"

"Are you quite sure about this, sweetheart?" said Sir John. "After all, these tournaments can be, well...awfully *violent* affairs, can't they?"

Now it was Thomas's turn to sigh. His father was the reason Thomas had never been to a tournament. Sir John was the least warlike knight in the kingdom. He hated anything to do with fighting, and much preferred reading old books or a quiet afternoon's fishing. Thomas loved his father, but he wished Sir John were more like the knights who won tournaments. It would be wonderful to have a father he could *really* look up to.

Mother opened her mouth to reply, but Matilda spoke before her.

"Er...hello?" she said, rolling her eyes at Thomas. "I think that's the whole point, Father. The knights won't be coming here to play games."

"Maybe they should," said Father. "They could play chess, although that might be hard for them. I know, how about draughts, or tiddlywinks..."

"Tiddlywinks?" said Matilda. "What's that? I've never heard of it."

"Well, each player has to flick these little counters—" said Sir John.

"*QUIET!*" yelled Lady Eleanor, glaring at them. "I might get violent myself if you don't shut up! It's going to be a *jousting* tournament, and that's the end of it. And just so there are no misunderstandings, let me make a few things absolutely clear. Matilda, you will *not* be entering – I simply couldn't allow a daughter of mine to do anything so unladylike."

"But...but..." Matilda spluttered. Lady Eleanor took no notice.

"And I'll definitely be keeping an eye on *you*, Thomas Bailey," she said, wagging a finger at her son. "If I get even the *slightest* hint that you're up to mischief, you'll be in *big* trouble, is that clear? Now, I've written out a list of tasks for each of you on these rolls of parchment..."

Thomas had already stopped listening.

Mischief? Him? As if! He was going to be far too busy enjoying himself to get up to any *mischief*.

Although, of course, you never knew *what* the future might hold...

Chapter Two

Encounter in the Woods

Thomas was standing outside the Keep, running his eyes up and down the list of tasks Mother had assigned to him. It included such thrilling items as tidying his bedchamber (which was mentioned twice), polishing the drawbridge chains, and helping Mouldy sweep out the stables. Sir John and Matilda were reading their lists, and all three of them were frowning. Sparky was lying in the courtyard nearby, his tail twitching nervously.

"I can't decide what's more depressing,"

muttered Thomas. "The fact that there's so much to do, or that everything on the list is so boring."

"At least you don't have to do all this awful *girly* stuff..." said Matilda. "I'll be spending most of my time before the tournament shopping with Mother, then I've got to run the stupid Snood Stall. And I can't believe she won't let me compete. You'll talk to her about it, Father, won't you?"

"I'll try, my lambkin," said Sir John, "but you know what your mother is like. Now, I think you two had better make a start on your lists. I might just pop into the kitchen for a bit of a snack before I set about mine..."

"You will do no such thing," snapped Lady Eleanor, sweeping out of the Keep and frowning at her husband. She had stayed in the Great Hall to give the servants their tasks. "What's the *first* item on your list?"

"Something about going on a, er...crash diet," Sir John said quietly, blushing and looking a little upset. "But I didn't think you meant it."

Thomas felt sorry for his father. Sir John was short and had always been rather plump. A crash diet was going to be very difficult for him.

"Well, I'm afraid I did," said Lady Eleanor. "I want us all to be looking our best for the tournament. Anyway, why are you three still here? You know what you're supposed to be doing, so off you go and do it."

"None of it's very interesting though, is it, Mother?" said Thomas. "I was wondering if I could help plan the actual events, the jousting."

"Hey, that's what I was going to ask!" said Matilda, pushing Thomas out of the way. "I've had this great idea for a special event with axes..."

"The answer to both of you is...no," said Lady Eleanor.

"But that's not fair!" whined Thomas and Matilda with a single voice.

"According to you I'm never fair," said Lady Eleanor. "So at least I'm consistent. Now, unless there's anything else, it's time to get busy."

"Huh, I absolutely *detest* being a child," Matilda muttered, turning round and sulkily stomping away. "Just you wait, one of these days..."

"Come on, Sparky," sighed Thomas, rolling up his parchment and stuffing it in a pocket. Sparky rose to his feet, ready to follow him.

"Actually, Sparky is staying with me," said Lady Eleanor.

"What for, Mother?" said Thomas. "I promise I won't let him start any more forest fires. And he gets terribly lonely when we're not together."

Sparky made his sad mooing noise again. He nudged Thomas and almost knocked him over, then looked pleadingly at Lady Eleanor.

"He'll be fine," she said briskly. "I've got plans for him, very interesting plans, as it happens. He can earn his keep for once instead of just costing us money. Right, this way, Sparky, and be quick about it."

Mother strode off before Thomas could say anything else. Sparky had listened carefully to

Mother and seemed to have understood her. He
had cheered up, anyway, and even seemed
rather excited. He nudged Thomas
once more, then scampered
along behind Lady Eleanor,
wagging his tail.

"Oh, great!" muttered Thomas. "Some friend *you* turned out to be, Sparky," he called out. "Thanks for all the loyalty...I *don't* think."

"Never mind, Tom," said Sir John, patting his son's shoulder. "There's not much Sparky could have done about it, is there? See you later."

Sir John hurried off. Thomas sighed, and thought about the first item on his list – sorting out a poster for the tournament. Mother had written down what it was supposed to say. His task was to get the monks at the local monastery's Scribe Shoppe to design it and make lots of copies. Mother wanted them put up all over the area as soon as possible.

Thomas trudged across the courtyard. The two men-at-arms were still at the gate, and someone else was with them now. Thomas saw it was Mouldy, his father's longest-serving man-at-arms. Lady Eleanor always maintained that Mouldy was the dimmest person in Creaky Castle. She was probably right, but Thomas liked the old soldier.

27

"Morning, Master Thomas," said Mouldy, saluting and grinning at him. The other two grinned as well. "Great news about the tournament, don't you think? Me and the lads are really looking forward to it."

"Morning, Mouldy," said Thomas without stopping. "Me too."

Of course it was wonderful news, he thought, heading down the path that led through the forest to the monastery. But it wasn't going to be any fun unless Mother lightened up a bit. He and Matilda had been right, she wasn't being fair. And what was all that about Sparky? The idea of her *having plans* for his pet dragon made Thomas feel rather worried...

At least the monks in the Scribe Shoppe were keen. Thomas thought it must have been because they never got much excitement – all that silence and praying was probably pretty dull. At any rate, they said they'd do the posters as a rush job, and would even get them put up.

So Thomas was soon heading back
home along the forest path. After a while
he turned a bend – and saw a boy carving
his initials on a tree with a knife.

"Hey, what do you
think you're up to?" Thomas
yelled at him. "You can't do
that, it's not allowed. This forest
belongs to my family!"

"Is that so?" drawled the boy, staring snootily
at him. "You're not much good at looking after it,
then. Half of it seems to have been burned down."

"That was an accident," snapped Thomas.
"Anyway, who are you?"

"Harry Fitzhooley," said the boy, slipping his knife into a sheath on his belt. *Fitzhooley*, thought Thomas... The name was familiar for some reason, but he couldn't remember why. "We've just moved into a castle on the other side of your *forest*," Harry continued. "Although if you ask me, it's more of a *copse*. We've got a much bigger wood on our land."

"Oh yeah?" said Thomas. He had taken an instant dislike to this boy. "I bet you haven't. And I bet my family has a lot more land than yours."

"Oh no, I don't think so," said Harry, giving him a superior smile. "I'm sure *my* family is much richer. In fact, my father is the most famous—"

"I don't care about your father, mine is..." Thomas said, and paused.

What was he going to say, that his father was short, plump and sweet-natured? That wouldn't score many points with someone like Harry Fitzhooley, would it? All at once Thomas found himself describing a very different man, the kind of father he wished he had. "My father is amazing, actually," he continued. "He's unstoppable with a lance, great with the sword or mace, he's tough, aggressive, a really fantastic jouster..."

Suddenly a large shadow fell across the two boys. Somebody had clanked into the clearing and was now standing directly behind Thomas.

"He sounds like a very talented man..." growled a deep voice.

Thomas slowly turned round...and gulped. The voice belonged to an enormous man, a knight clad head to toe in armour so black it somehow seemed to suck the light from the sky. He had fists the size of boulders and the cold green eyes of a hungry wolf in winter.

"Er...hello, Father," Harry said nervously, and Thomas recalled where he'd heard Harry's surname before. There was a *Top Thumps* card

about a certain Sir Richard Fitzhooley, otherwise
known as the Dark Knight.

Could this be the same jousting hero? It certainly
looked like him...

Chapter Three

A Terrible Vision

Thomas could see the card in his mind now. As the Dark Knight, Sir Richard Fitzhooley was one of the most successful tournament fighters of all time. He had won dozens of events and was notorious for being incredibly violent, utterly merciless, and a real stickler for the rules.

"He's the Dark Knight, right?" said Thomas. "And he's your *dad*?"

Harry shrugged, and nodded. Thomas was thrilled to be in the presence of a genuine celebrity, and wondered if he dare ask for an autograph.

"Harry," rumbled Sir Richard. "Where have you been? I've been searching all over for you."

"I...I was on my way home, Father, honest," Harry said, nervously. "I'm only late because this stupid boy wouldn't stop talking."

"Hey, who are you calling stupid?" said Thomas, offended.

"My son can call anyone stupid if he wants to," growled Sir Richard, looming darkly over Thomas. "Do you have a problem with that, boy?"

"No, I don't..." said Thomas, slightly taken aback by Sir Richard's breath, which was very bad, and also by his aggression. But then he told himself it was quite natural for a father to stand up for his son...

"I'm glad," said Sir Richard, leaning a little closer, the almost visible cloud of his breath starting to make Thomas feel rather faint. "Now tell me, who is *your* father?" said Sir Richard. "And where do you live?

"Er...my father is Sir John Bailey," said Thomas. "We live in Creaky Castle, and you might be interested to hear we're about to put on a—"

"Umm, never heard of him," growled Sir Richard. He frowned, and his thick, bristling eyebrows crashed into each other like a couple of angry boars. "But judging by what you said, he's the kind of opponent I enjoy fighting. So I'll remember the name, and I will *definitely* challenge him if we ever meet. Come along, Harry, your mother sent me to fetch you. It's time for lunch." Sir Richard strode off, his feet thudding on the path.

"Yes, Father!" said Harry, and he scampered along after him, pausing only to stick his tongue out at Thomas. Normally Thomas would have returned the favour, but he was happy just to see the Fitzhooleys depart. Meeting the Dark Knight had been awesome. He was certainly scary, his bad breath alone could knock you out – and even his own son seemed afraid of him. But Thomas rather wished he hadn't told that whacking great fib about Father being such an amazing jouster.

He had a nasty feeling that if he'd finished what he'd been going to say about the Creaky Castle Tournament, Sir Richard would already be on his way to sign up for it...and challenge Father!

A terrible vision popped into his mind – the Dark Knight thundering down the jousting course on a huge, snorting warhorse, his deadly lance pointed straight at poor old Sir John. There was no way Father could stand up to a professional jouster like Sir Richard Fitzhooley. The Dark Knight would chop him into little bits. And if that happened, it would be Thomas's fault...

Thomas shook his head, and the vision vanished. Father wasn't daft enough to accept a challenge from Sir Richard. He could just refuse. Or at least Thomas hoped he could. Of course, it depended on what it said in the official rule book. Jousting was a sport with lots of rules, but Thomas hadn't bothered to learn them all, being more interested in the fighting statistics and the prowess of the *Top Thumps* knights. However, he did vaguely remember some of them being quite strange. What if the Dark Knight could *force* Father to fight him?

Thomas felt his blood turn cold again. He needed to find out if he had really put Father at risk – and the quickest way to do that would be to ask Matilda. She was always studying the jousting rule book, and could even quote it in detail. He'd have to be careful how he raised the subject, though. He didn't want anyone to know there might be...well, a problem.

After hurrying back to Creaky Castle, where things were already changing, Thomas walked through the gate and saw men-at-arms and servants bustling around. Some were removing the old carts and cleaning up the rubbish that usually cluttered the courtyard, while others were building a low wooden fence, with lots of hammering and banging and shouting.

Then, Thomas realized it wasn't a fence, and his heart leaped with excitement again.

It was The Tilt, an essential part of
the jousting course, the wooden wall
that divided the knights as they
charged each other! The rest of the
course was being laid out too.

A servant was painting white lines,
and a team of men was putting up
a bank of seats for all the spectators.

"Hey there, little brother," said Matilda, coming up beside him. "It's not looking bad so far, is it? Although I only hope they get everything right."

"Yeah, I, er...hope they do too, sis," said Thomas, trying to sound every bit as concerned as she did. "I mean, it's like...*so* important."

"That's what I told Mother," muttered Matilda with a scowl. "But she won't listen to me. I don't

think she's even *opened* the rule book I gave her."

"Actually, it's funny you should mention the rules," said Thomas. "I wanted to ask you something. Er...what if a knight at a tournament decided to challenge the lord of the castle where it was being held? The lord doesn't *have* to accept the challenge if he doesn't want to, does he?"

"That's a very...*technical* question for you," said Matilda, surprised. She gave him a suspicious look. "Why do you want to know, anyway?"

"Oh, er...no particular reason," squeaked Thomas. "I just wondered."

"Really?" said Matilda. "Oh well, let me see... I think it's pretty much covered by Rule 117, Section 3, Subsection 24... *Should a competing knight challenge the lord of the castle or any other such venue where a jousting tournament is being held, the lord must immediately accept the challenge or forfeit all his lands, wealth and the said castle forthwith, and shall then in addition be hanged by the neck until he is dead...*"

"*WHAT?!*" yelped Thomas, his eyes suddenly wide with horror.

"Whoa, calm down," said Matilda, and she laughed. "Oh, I get it, you're worried about Father! Well, it won't happen at *our* tournament. It's a very old rule, and the last time anybody invoked it was hundreds of years ago. I'd guess most knights don't even know it's still in the rule book. They'll all be coming to compete for the prize money, anyway. It wouldn't even occur to them to think that the castle itself could be up for grabs."

"Thank goodness," muttered Thomas. "Er...not that I *was* worried about it happening at our tournament, of course," he added quickly.

"Mind you," said Matilda, looking thoughtful, "I suppose someone who was a real stickler for the rules might try and use it some day." Then she smiled. "But what are the chances of that? Anyway, see you later."

Matilda hurried away, and Thomas stood rooted to the spot, oblivious to the bustle around him.

An image of Sir Richard
filled his mind, the one from
his *Top Thumps* card, the
Dark Knight standing
with a foot on the chest
of a defeated knight.
And Thomas couldn't
stop thinking about the
description on the card:
*The Dark Knight is a
stickler for the rules.*

44

Thomas felt sick. If Sir Richard did hear about their tournament, Father might soon be facing a very unpleasant choice – one between giving up Creaky Castle and everything they had, or getting slaughtered by the Dark Knight. Suddenly a crazy idea popped into Thomas's head.

He could always make sure the tournament didn't take place...

Chapter Four

Voice from the Sky

That was easier said than done, of course.

The simplest thing would be to persuade Mother the tournament just wasn't a good idea. But Thomas quickly decided there wasn't much point in trying that approach. It wasn't likely that Mother would listen to him, and what would he say, anyway? Telling the truth would definitely get him into *SERIOUS* trouble.

He had to come up with some other way of stopping the tournament, though. He stood in the bustling courtyard, thinking hard, his face screwed up with the effort. His mind, however, stubbornly stayed blank. He needed more time. Then, with a sudden surge of panic, he remembered the posters. He would have to return to the Scribe Shoppe and make sure the order was cancelled!

Thomas turned round and ran towards the main gate, dodging servants with brooms and men-at-arms carrying planks. He dashed out of the castle and along the path towards the woods. He hadn't gone far when he saw something that made him skid to a halt.

A large poster had been pasted onto one of the trees:

Entries invited for a
Grand Jousting Tournament

to be staged this weekend at fabulous
Creaky Castle

Cash prize for Tournament winner
Low entry fees • Other attractions
Food stalls

Families and coach parties welcome

Don't delay • enter today

Thomas had to admit the monks at the Scribe Shoppe had done a great job. The poster featured a terrific picture of two knights jousting, and the lettering was clear. Way *too* clear as far as Thomas was concerned. There was only one thing for it. He picked at a corner and tried to pull the poster off. But it remained firmly – and very annoyingly – stuck to the trunk.

"Thomas Bailey, what *do* you think you're doing?" said a familiar voice. Strangely enough, it seemed to be coming from the sky.

Thomas looked up. Mother hadn't learned to fly, although he wouldn't have put it past her. She was looking down at him from the battlements above the castle gate. Beside her two men-at-arms were wrestling with a huge banner that said *CREAKY CASTLE – HOME OF THE JOUST*. Thomas guessed they were trying to hang it over the portcullis, with Mother there to keep an eye on them.

"I was, er...just straightening it, Mother," said Thomas, snatching his hand from the poster as if it were red-hot and he'd been scorched. "I thought it was a bit crooked, and I know you like things to be perfect."

"Are you *quite* sure about that, Thomas?"
Mother said, her eyes narrowed. "It looked to me
more like you were trying to pull it off."

"Oh no, Mother, I definitely wasn't doing *that*,"
Thomas replied, his fingers crossed behind his
back. "Why would I want to, anyway?"

"I have no idea," said Mother, "especially as you seem to have done an excellent job in sorting out the posters. They're just what I had in mind, and the Scribe Shoppe has been so quick! I spoke to the monk who put that one up, and he said they'd be everywhere by the end of the day."

"Oh, *great*," muttered Thomas. "Er...I mean, that's terrific, Mother. Well, I'm afraid I can't hang around chatting. I still have *masses* to do..."

Thomas smiled, gave her a cheery wave, and started to sidle away. If he hurried, he might be able to catch the monk putting up the posters and stop him. If he couldn't, well, he would simply have to try and tear down as many as possible. Mother, however, hadn't finished with him yet.

"Actually, Thomas, there's no need to rush off. I've got another important job for you. You'd better come back into the castle."

"But...but..." Thomas spluttered, trying to think of something to say, tempted just to run for it. There was no escape, though, and he knew it.

"What is it with you and your sister and that word?" said Mother. "Read my lips – inside, and get a move on! And what's taking you men so long?" she snarled. "Hanging out a banner can't possibly be *that* hard!

Mother turned away, not realizing that she'd

startled one of the
men-at-arms, who became
hopelessly entangled in one
of the banner's ropes and
fell over the wall with
a scream. Thomas
hurried in through the
gate, dodging past the
man dangling upside down,
too distracted to take much notice.
The other man-at-arms was already
hauling his
mate back up.

"Stay calm," Thomas
murmured to himself. "I *must* stay calm."

He knew he would have to hide his anxiety
from Mother – the last thing he needed was for
her to get suspicious. But panic was bubbling
inside him now. He didn't have much time. Every
second that passed meant there was more chance
of the Dark Knight seeing a poster.

"Right, Thomas, follow me," said Mother, coming down the last few steps from the wall and striding off across the courtyard. Thomas scuttled after her. "This won't take long – to explain, that is. You might well have to spend the rest of the day working on it, though."

"The rest of the *day*..." Thomas started to moan. But he quickly got himself under control. "What about all the other things on my list?"

"Oh, don't worry about them," Mother said airily. "In fact, you can forget your list. This takes priority over everything. Ah, here we are."

Mother came to a halt in a far corner of the courtyard, the one she had been looking at earlier when she had caught Thomas unawares.

A strange contraption stood there now. Two Y-shaped metal poles had been stuck in the ground, and a straight

pole placed across them at head height. There was
a handle on the end of the straight pole, and what
appeared to be a lump of something charred and
blackened impaled in the middle of it.

Thomas realized the contraption was a spit for
roasting meat outdoors. Mouldy was holding the
handle, looking nervous and slightly singed in
various places, while Sparky lay beyond. The
dragon was obviously pleased to see Thomas.
He leaped to his feet and bounded
over, wagging his tail
ecstatically and sending
a couple of passing
servants flying.

"Give over, Sparky, you can't get round me like that," muttered Thomas as his pet nuzzled him with his huge snout. But soon Thomas was stroking his scaly hide, much to the dragon's pleasure. "Oh, go on then, I forgive you," said Thomas. "What have you been doing, anyway?"

"I've been trying to make him barbecue some meat," Mother said crossly. "You gave me the idea when I heard you talking about roasting chestnuts. A Dragon Kebab Stall would be a terrific attraction and bring in a lot of extra money. The trouble is that he doesn't seem to understand what I want. So as he's *your* pet, I decided *you* could teach him, okay?"

"Er...I'm not sure I understand what you want, either," said Thomas.

"You managed to barbecue half a forest between you, so I'm sure you'll work it out," replied Mother. "Mouldy will fill you in on the details. Hello, who's that? Wonderful, I think we might have our first entry!"

Thomas looked round – and for the third time that day his blood ran cold. A huge, snorting warhorse was coming through the castle gateway.

And riding it was the Dark Knight.

Chapter Five

Searching for Prey

Thomas watched Sir Richard trotting across the courtyard on his horse, scattering servants and men-at-arms before him and finally halting near the Keep. The knight dismounted and looked around, his helmeted head slowly swivelling like that of a huge black hawk searching for prey.

Thomas slipped behind Sparky and peeked from beneath the dragon's snout, his heart sinking. He realized there was no point now in trying to prevent the posters from being put up. Mother was right – Sir Richard must already have seen one, and had come to enter the tournament.

"Well, I'll leave you to it, Thomas," said Mother, and she hurried off, cutting her own swathe through the servants and soldiers. Many of them had stopped work and were gawping at Sir Richard. A few sharp words of encouragement from Lady Eleanor soon had them jumping.

"Thank goodness you're taking charge here, Master Thomas," said Mouldy the instant she was out of earshot. "I mean, don't get me wrong or anything, Her Ladyship is a wonderful woman, of course. But she has absolutely no idea how to handle a dragon. She kept telling him what to do, and the louder she shouted, the more excited she made him..."

"Really?" Thomas murmured, barely listening to Mouldy's chatter. He was too busy trying to work out what was happening over by the Keep. Mother was talking to Sir Richard, probably welcoming him to Creaky Castle... He saw Sir Richard say something in reply, Mother pulling a face and quickly leaning back from him.

"Oh yes," Mouldy was saying. "He did his best, the poor creature – didn't you, Sparky?" The dragon gave a sad little moo. "But he just can't seem to get the size of the flame right. Either he leaves the meat almost raw or he burns it to a complete crisp. And he definitely has a problem with his aim as well. He nearly roasted *me* alive a couple of times..."

"Is that so?" muttered Thomas. Lady Eleanor was still talking, and Thomas was beginning to think it might be okay. Perhaps Sir Richard would simply pay his entry fee and leave. After all, he hadn't seemed much like the chatty sort in the forest, had he? But to Thomas's dismay,

Mother gestured to the doors of the Keep – and led Sir Richard inside.

"Anyway, I'm sure you'll be able to sort him out, Master Thomas," said Mouldy. "Her Ladyship has plans for other attractions along here – more food stalls, one selling tournament scarves and Creaky Castle souvenirs, maybe even a booth where you can bet on the competitors. But she's pinning most of her hopes on Sparky and the Dragon Kebab Stall..."

"Listen, Mouldy, I've, er...got to go and talk to Mother," muttered Thomas. "I won't be long. Sparky, you're to stay with Mouldy, okay?"

Thomas ignored Sparky's plaintive moan and ran off towards the Keep. By the time he caught up with Mother and Sir Richard, they were in the Great Hall. The door was ajar, and Thomas peered round it.

Things had changed in the Great Hall too. The dining table had been pushed over to one side, and hanging on the wall above it was a big sign saying *COMPETITORS' REGISTRATION*. The ink pot and quill pen were on the table as before, but next to them now were a large leather-bound ledger and a strongbox with a lock and key. Mother was sitting behind the table, and Sir Richard was standing in front of her. Thomas saw her open the ledger and pick up the quill, then look at Sir Richard and smile.

"So, let me see, it's Sir Richard Fitzhooley, fighting as..." she said.

"The Dark Knight," rumbled Sir Richard, his voice like thunder.

"Umm, what a very...striking name," said Mother, writing it down in the ledger. "I'm delighted to have you as our first registered competitor. The entry fee is ten gold pieces – payable in cash upfront, I'm afraid."

"As you wish," growled Sir Richard, tossing a purse onto the table. It landed with a dull chink and several gold coins rolled out. "I take it you are the lady of the castle, and that your husband is Sir John Bailey..."

Thomas suddenly felt his heart hammering at his ribs. He didn't like the way this was going, but he couldn't just walk over and butt in. After all, he was supposed to be outside teaching Sparky how to cook meat, not hanging around indoors. And what if Sir Richard revealed that they'd met earlier in the forest? Things could get very awkward. Thomas crossed his fingers and hoped Sir Richard wouldn't say anything else.

"Yes, that's right," said Lady Eleanor, putting the money into the strongbox and locking it, slipping

the key into her own purse. "Is there any particular reason why you ask?" she added, looking puzzled.

Oh no, thought Thomas. Why did Mother have to go and say that? He needed to stop this conversation before it went any further. Suddenly an idea popped into his head, something *he* could say that might well do the trick. He pushed the door wide open and hurried into the hall.

"As a matter of fact there is," Sir Richard growled. He placed his fist on the table and leaned forward

on his knuckles. Lady Eleanor's nostrils quivered, and she went quite pale. "I wish to meet Sir John so I can–"

"Hey, hold on a minute!" yelled Thomas, dashing over and skidding to a stop by the dining table. "I, er...have a suggestion to make, Mother."

"How many times have I told you it's rude to interrupt, Thomas?" said Mother crossly, giving him one of her special glares. "What are you doing here, anyway? I gave you strict orders to concentrate on working with Sparky, so run along before I *really* lose my temper. I apologize for my son, Sir Richard. You were talking about my husband, I believe—"

"I'm sorry for interrupting," Thomas said quickly. Mother opened her mouth to say something, but Thomas just kept talking. "I wanted to let you know that I'd be happy to show the competitors round the castle and grounds. I'm sure we could offer tours at a *very reasonable price.*"

Mother raised that stern eyebrow again, and for a second Thomas thought his ploy hadn't worked. But her face took on a thoughtful look, and then she smiled, her eyes gleaming. She turned back to Sir Richard.

"How about it, Sir Richard?" she said. "Would you like a tour? As you're our very first entrant we could offer you a special discount."

"No tour," growled Sir Richard. "*I wish to meet Sir John Bailey.*"

He kept his eyes fixed on Lady Eleanor, who

leaned back to avoid the foul-smelling gale of his bad breath.

"Well, if you insist," murmured Lady Eleanor. Sir Richard gave her a curt nod, and she frowned. "Go and find your father, Thomas," she said.

"Er...I'm pretty sure he's just gone down to the village," said Thomas, thinking quickly. "He still hasn't managed to do all the things on his list."

"In that case, tell Bailey I will see him at the tournament," bellowed Sir Richard, standing up straight. "And that I am looking forward to it." Then he stomped off, his thudding footsteps making the whole hall shake.

"Well, *he* wasn't very nice, was he?" said Lady Eleanor, waving her hand in front of her face. "I hope none of the other competitors will be like him. And I can't understand why he's so keen to meet your father." She gave her son a searching stare. "Do *you* have any idea, Thomas?"

"What – me, Mother?" said Thomas. "Er...no, I haven't got a clue..."

Chapter Six

A Rock and a Hard Place

Thomas stood in front of Mother, caught in her steely gaze, unable to move. He knew she was testing him. Sometimes all she had to do was stare into his eyes and wait a while, and he would suddenly find himself confessing to every single crime he was keeping secret from her.

But he couldn't let that happen now. He resisted, doing his utmost to look innocent, and after a few difficult seconds Mother gave a sigh.

"Well, we'll find out eventually," she said. "I

can't worry about it – even though I have a feeling you're hiding something. But I'll let you off because I like your tour idea. I'm pretty sure that some of the other competitors will go for it. How much do you think we can charge?"

"Oh, er...five gold pieces," replied Thomas, trying to sound confident. "We could offer tours to everybody as a special deal with their tickets."

"Yes, you're right..." said Mother, her eyes gleaming again. "I'm glad to see you obviously take more after me than your father where this kind of thing is concerned. Mind you, I still expect that dragon of yours to be fully barbecue-trained by the end of the day. Is that clear, Thomas?"

"Er...absolutely, Mother," stammered Thomas. "I'd better get back to it."

Thomas hurried out of the Keep and across the courtyard. Mouldy and Sparky were where he'd left them, but Father and Matilda were there now, too, plus a couple of servants unloading a cart.

Thomas saw it contained a great heap of raw meat – more samples for Sparky to practise on.

"Hello, Thomas," Father said cheerily. "Just thought I'd check on you, see how you're getting on." He paused, his eyes drifting towards the large lump of meat Mouldy was struggling to get onto the skewer. "I say, that looks like it will cook up a treat. These kebabs are going to be *so* tasty..."

"Oh, give it a rest, Father," moaned Matilda, who then turned to Thomas. "He's done nothing but talk about food ever since Mother used the 'd' word on him. Anyone would think he was starving to death, but it's only a few hours since he had breakfast. And it will be lunchtime soon."

"Huh, I can't wait," Sir John said glumly. "I'll probably be getting a couple of lettuce leaves. Still, mustn't grumble. I'll do whatever it takes to make your mother happy. Is it right that we've already had an entrant, Tom?"

"Yes, Father," Thomas said reluctantly. "Sir Richard Fitzhooley..."

"Wow, I *don't* believe it," said Matilda. "The Dark Knight himself!"

"Splendid!" said Father. "Er...I take it you think he's pretty good?"

"Good?" said Matilda. "He's the best there is. I mean, his record in tournaments is terrific, isn't it, Tom? He's consistently top of the Premier League. I can't wait to see him in action."

"Me too," said Father. Matilda and Thomas looked at him in surprise. "No, I mean it, I really do. This tournament is very important to your mother, so I fully intend to get into the spirit of things. We'll have the best seats, after all, so it might feel almost as if I'm taking part myself."

Nobody except Sparky seemed to notice Thomas let out a small squeak. The dragon crept over to Thomas, gave him a gentle nudge with his huge, smoky snout, and looked at him with big, worried eyes.

"Come on, Father, I want to show you Tom's *Top Thumps* collection," said Matilda with a grin. "We'll make a tournament fan of you yet. Is that okay with you, Tom? I promise I won't lose any or get them out of order."

"Sure, no problem," Thomas murmured. "They're under my bed."

"I know where they are," said Matilda with a wink. "See you later!"

Thomas watched his father and sister stroll away, smiling and talking. They wouldn't be so cheerful if they knew what was in store, he thought, deep gloom seeping through his mind like the long shadow of the Dark Knight falling over him in the forest. It was all going to be a disaster.

"Cheer up, Master Thomas," said Mouldy. He had got the meat onto the skewer and balanced it on the uprights, and the servants had left with the empty cart. "Now I was wondering if *you'd* like to turn the handle..."

"What I'd like is to discover I'd never been born," Thomas moaned, "or that someone could wave a magic wand and get me out of this mess."

"Why, what's wrong?" asked Mouldy, surprised. "Can *I* help?"

Thomas opened his mouth to say no, he didn't think so, but then he paused. Mouldy's face was full of concern, and Thomas suddenly felt he couldn't keep everything bottled up inside any more. He would explode if he did... So he started talking, telling Mouldy about what he'd done – and what he thought was certain to happen on the day of the tournament.

"Umm, I see your problem," said Mouldy at last. "You're kind of stuck between a rock and a hard place, aren't you? Either you tell Her Ladyship and get yourself in a *world* of trouble, especially if it means she has to cancel the tournament. Or you keep quiet and your dad gets it in the neck. And just about everywhere else if what I've heard about Sir Richard is right. Someone told me at his last tournament he cut off a knight's—"

"Er...you can stop there, Mouldy," Thomas said quickly, wincing and holding up a hand. "I don't want to hear it. The question is, what do I *do*?"

"Ah, sorry, can't help you there, Master Thomas..." said Mouldy, shaking his head. Sparky glanced at the old soldier, then back at Thomas, and gave a pathetic little moo. "It's funny you should mention magic wands, though," Mouldy continued. "I do know somebody who's got one, a wizard by the name of Faldor. He makes pretty good magic potions, too – I bought one myself recently. A lot of people round here use them."

"Really?" asked Thomas, suddenly interested. "Er...what for?"

"Oh, the usual stuff," said Mouldy. "Getting rid of warts and boils, curing dandruff, that sort of thing. But he does much stronger potions as well, or at least that's what he claims. You know, the kind they have in the old stories – one drop and you're turned into a frog, or you fall asleep for a hundred years, or an enemy's strength suddenly vanishes, or–"

"Whoa, hold on a minute!" said Thomas, his mind racing. "That last one sounds perfect! If we could somehow use a potion like that on Sir Richard maybe Father would survive even if he *did* have to fight him! What do you think, Mouldy – is this Faldor the real deal? Can he do it?"

"Why don't we go and ask him?" said Mouldy. "He lives on the other side of the forest. We could probably be there and back in an hour or so."

"But what about Sparky and the barbecue?" said Thomas. "Mother will kill me if she comes to check up on things and sees that I'm not here."

"Ah, well, I think Her Ladyship might be very busy herself for the next few hours, Master Thomas," said Mouldy. "Just take a look at that lot." He nodded in the direction of the castle gate.

Thomas turned and saw a line of knights trotting through to register, at least twenty, maybe more.

Thomas smiled. There was a chance things might be fine after all...

Chapter Seven

Meeting the Wizard

Thomas thought Faldor's cottage was far too ordinary to be the home of a wizard. It was small and scruffy, with white smoke rising from a crooked chimney. But as Thomas and Mouldy approached, Sparky trailing along behind them, the smoke turned green, then orange, and finally purple.

Mouldy grinned at Thomas, and turned to knock on the cottage door. It opened before he touched it, a raven flying out with a loud squawk.

A tall, thin man who could only be the wizard

stood in the doorway. Faldor had a long, straggly white beard and a huge shock of pure white hair that pointed upwards and outwards. He was wearing a shabby, dark-blue gown embroidered with faded moons and stars and strange designs. And he was staring at Thomas and Mouldy, his eyes rolling wildly.

"What is it?" he snapped. "If you've come to complain about that plague of poisonous toads in the village, it's got nothing to do with me."

"Poisonous toads?" said Mouldy, confused. "Er...no, that's not why we're here at all. Don't you remember me? I came to you for a magic potion a couple of weeks ago, and I have to say it worked a treat."

"Oh yes, it's...Mouldy, isn't it?" said Faldor. "Glad to hear from a satisfied customer. Nasty place to have a boil, though, right on your—"

"I've brought young Master Thomas from up at the castle this time," Mouldy said hurriedly. "He needs help with something, er...serious."

"You'd better come in then," said Faldor, peering at Thomas, who smiled uncertainly. "You'll have to leave your dragon outside, though."

Sparky seemed happily occupied watching the coloured smoke rise from the chimney, so Thomas followed Mouldy in. There was only a single room, its walls lined with dusty shelves, each full of jars containing weird things – glittering powders and liquids, pickled rats and spiders, even one crammed with eyeballs. There was a table in the middle, and scattered on it were some old books and parchments, and a wand.

"Now, young man," said Faldor. "What seems to be the trouble?"

"Well, it's like this..." said Thomas, and he told Faldor everything. "So I need to save my father," he murmured at last. "And Mouldy said you might have a potion that could make Sir Richard's strength vanish."

"Let me see..." said Faldor, flicking through one of the books on the table. "Love potions, hate

potions, toad potions...actually, you can forget I
said that... Ah, here we are. This one definitely
ought to do the trick. As soon as this Sir Richard
drinks my fabulous, unique Opposites Potion, it
will instantly change all his qualities into their
opposites. His bravery will become fear, his strength
weakness, and so on. How does that sound?"

"It sounds absolutely perfect," said Thomas with a grin. But then he frowned. "Hey, hang on a second – how do I get him to drink it?"

"Not my problem, I'm afraid," Faldor said briskly, and he started taking down jars. "Anyway, I could have a batch ready for you by teatime. I've got everything I need...newt's tongue...viper venom...unicorn spit... And I can offer you a bargain price, too. Shall we say...fifty gold pieces?"

"*How much?*" squeaked Thomas. "I haven't got that kind of money!"

"Hard luck, then," snapped Faldor, slamming shut his book of spells. A cloud of ancient dust rose from it. He scowled and started putting the jars back in their places. "No cash, no potion. Now if you'll excuse me..."

"I could always lend you a bit, Master Thomas," said Mouldy, digging into the purse on his belt and pulling out a few coins. "I haven't got much, only a farthing and a couple of groats, but it's yours if you need it."

"Thanks, Mouldy, I think I'll be okay," murmured Thomas. Mouldy had in fact given him an idea, although it was one that made Thomas feel uncomfortable. Mouldy's purse had reminded him of another purse he'd seen recently – the one in which Mother kept the key to her strongbox.

Thomas turned back to Faldor. "Can we bring the money later?"

"Of course," said Faldor, smiling. "Your potion will be waiting..."

Thomas brooded all the way back to Creaky Castle. He thought there was probably plenty of money in Mother's strongbox now, certainly enough to pay for the potion. But he couldn't simply walk up to her and ask for fifty gold pieces, could he? So he would have to take – no, *steal* it.

Just thinking about doing it made him feel scared, and very guilty.

Deep down he was still hoping for a miracle – maybe Sir Richard would change his mind about challenging Father. But Thomas also felt he needed the potion, in case he couldn't prevent the worst from happening. He would worry about the consequences later, when Father was saved. And he would find a way of paying back the money somehow...

Doing the actual deed itself turned out to be easier than he'd expected. He left Mouldy and Sparky at the Kebab Stall and slipped inside the Keep. He made for the chamber Mother was using as her office. Mother wasn't there – but her purse was lying on the table next to the strongbox.

Thomas crept in, and the money was soon in his pocket. He locked the strongbox, put the key back in Mother's purse, then turned to leave.

Mother suddenly appeared in the doorway, blocking his escape.

"What are you doing in here, Thomas?" she said, frowning at him.

"Me, Mother?" he said. He could feel himself blushing. "I was, er...looking for you to see if there was anything else I could do to help."

"Really?" said Mother. "Have you got Sparky sorted out, then?"

"Of course," said Thomas, fingers crossed behind his back, a sense of impending doom settling on him. Mother put a hand on the strongbox.

"You know, Thomas," she said, "you've behaved strangely a couple of times today, even for you, and usually that would make me suspicious." She paused and, much to Thomas's surprise...she smiled. "But I'm going to give you the benefit of the doubt, and assume you're just stressed like the rest of us. You're being such a good boy, and I am *so* proud of you."

"Er...thanks, Mother," Thomas mumbled. "I'm not being *that* good."

"Oh, that's not true," said Mother. "I can tell you

realize just how important this tournament is for the family, for me and your father..."

Moments later Thomas left the Keep feeling guiltier than ever. The coins felt heavy in his pocket, weighing it down like a terrible sin, and he was relieved to hand them over to Mouldy. The old soldier hurried off to Faldor immediately, and soon returned, meeting Thomas in the stables.

"I've got the potion," he said, grinning. He gave Thomas a small glass flask containing a thick green liquid. Thomas thought it looked like one of those disgusting healthy soups Mother was always trying to get him to eat. "There's even some change for you," Mouldy continued proudly.

"I haggled, and Faldor knocked a couple of gold pieces off the price."

"You'd better hang on to it for the time being," said Thomas. Putting a couple of coins back in the strongbox wasn't worth the risk. Mother had almost caught him the first time, so he would wait until he had all fifty pieces to return.

"Oh, right," said Mouldy, and he briefly looked thoughtful. "What do you want me to do now, Master Thomas? I'm sure you must have a plan."

"Actually, Mouldy, I'm still working on it..." Thomas murmured.

And if he was to be honest, he wasn't getting very far, either...

Chapter Eight

The Tournament Begins

Two days later, on a bright, sunny Saturday morning, Thomas stood in the courtyard observing a scene that should have filled his heart with joy. Everything was ready – the jousting course, the knights' pavilions, the special attractions and stalls – and a huge crowd was flowing steadily into Creaky Castle. All he could do, however, was bite his lip with worry.

The tournament was scheduled to start soon, and he was supposed to be taking his seat. Yet he still

hadn't come up with a way of tricking Sir Richard
into drinking the potion. In fact he'd only had one
idea, which was to slip it into a goblet of wine –
Mother had arranged for the competitors to be
given refreshments – but the potion was too thick
and green for that.

There was another problem, too, one Thomas
had been struggling with. He had to admit that the
shine had been taken off his dream just a little.
Meeting a lot of his heroes on the guided tours of
the castle had turned out to be something of a
disappointment. In the flesh, most of them were
loud, nasty and totally wrapped up in themselves.
And the Dark Knight was the most unpleasant of
them all.

At that moment, Sir Richard was standing
outside his pavilion with his wife, Lady Fitzhooley,
and their children, Harry and his little sister. Lady
Fitzhooley was thin and pale, and she and the
children looked bored and unhappy. Thomas felt
quite sorry for them, even though Harry had just

made a face at him. Sir Richard seemed to shout
at them continually.

No wonder Harry had been so nervous when his
father had found him in the forest that day. If Sir
Richard was like that at home, too, then he must
be really difficult to live with, and not much of a
dad, either...

Just then a knight galloped past Thomas, heading for the practice area, his horse's hooves thundering, his armour gleaming in the sun. Thomas watched him, and shook his head to clear out the negative thoughts.

"Get a grip!" he hissed to himself. What did it matter if Sir Richard and the others weren't nice?

They were fantastic fighters, and that was what counted. Who cared about being nice and polite? There was going to be *a tournament* here, in his own backyard! It was something to look forward to, not moan about. The jousting would be awesome, and there was still time to save Father. Why, Sir Richard hadn't even challenged him yet...

Thomas squared his shoulders and went to join his family, determined to think of a way to get Sir Richard to drink the potion if he needed to. Mother, Father and a grumpy-looking Matilda were in their places. The Baileys' seats were in the best position, on the halfway line of the jousting course.

"Ah, there you are, Thomas," said Mother. "I was about to send a search party for you. Is everything okay with Sparky and Mouldy?"

"Er...yes, Mother, I'm sure it is," said Thomas, trying to sound convincing. He glanced over at the Dragon Kebab Stall and saw that a queue had already formed, although Sparky hadn't begun cooking yet. Mouldy saw Thomas looking, and waved. Sparky wagged his tail. At least things should be okay there, Thomas thought. He and Mouldy had worked hard with Sparky, and surprisingly enough the dragon seemed quite good at cooking now. They'd only had a couple of accidents during Sparky's training, when he'd been distracted by something or got overexcited. He would be fine so long as he concentrated on the job.

"Good, I'm glad," said Mother, an anxious expression on her face. "We really need them to do well today. I hadn't realized how much it costs to put on this kind of event, and that's not even counting the prize money we'll have to pay out. At this rate we'll be pushed to make any profit."

Suddenly, Father's tummy gave off several strange rumbling noises, and he blushed. "Er...sorry about that, everyone," he murmured. "This crash diet has done terrible things to my stomach. I feel hungry all the time... Anyway, relax, dear. The tournament is bound to be a success."

"I almost hope it isn't," Matilda muttered, hunching down in her seat and scowling at Mother. "I still can't believe I'm not allowed to enter."

"And I can't believe you're still whingeing on about it!" snapped Mother. "The answer is no, young lady, and that really is the end of it."

"Girls, girls!" Father hissed. "I think it's time we got started."

"Quite right," Mother replied, standing up to address the crowd. Behind her Matilda stuck out her tongue, and sulked. "Good morning, everybody," said Mother, and the buzz of noise in the courtyard faded. "Welcome to the very first Jousting Tournament here at Creaky Castle..." She outlined the programme for the day, and asked the competitors to step forward.

A line of knights in full armour came clanking
onto the jousting course and waved to the crowd.
A herald called out their names and the crowd
cheered each one, saving the biggest cheer of all
for the Dark Knight.

"Well, I'm sure we're in for some really, er...keen contests," said Mother. "So let's get this show on the road. The first bout is between—"

"You can stop there!" Sir Richard roared suddenly, his voice booming out round the courtyard. "I have something rather important to say."

The crowd fell silent again, and Sir Richard marched ominously towards the Baileys. Thomas groaned, and sat bolt upright in his seat. It looked like he was about to run out of time, and there was absolutely nothing he could do about it. Sir Richard finally clanked to a halt.

"*Sir John Bailey...*" he cried, "*I hereby challenge you to a joust!*"

There were gasps of surprise from the crowd, and some screams.

"I'm sorry, Sir Richard, but you must be confused," said Lady Eleanor. "Sir John isn't competing today, so I'm afraid you can't challenge him."

"But I *can*," growled Sir Richard. "I have a right to challenge the lord of this castle under Rule 117, Section 3, Subsection 24 of the rule book..."

"What *is* he talking about?" Mother whispered. "Have you got any idea, Matilda? You're the one who's always going on about the rule book."

"Oh no, I don't believe this is happening," Matilda groaned, her sulking forgotten now. "I hate to tell you, Mother, but he *does* have the right."

She suddenly seemed to remember something, and turned to look at Thomas with her eyes narrowed. Thomas gulped, and avoided her gaze.

"Oh, don't be ridiculous, Matilda," Mother said, then scowled. "I'm warning you all, this had better not be some kind of practical joke."

"I assure you it's not," snarled Sir Richard. "I'm *deadly* serious..."

A bad-tempered discussion began, Sir Richard
growling and Mother getting more and more cross.
Other competitors joined in the debate, and even
some of the crowd, although Father stayed silent.
The rule book was consulted, and Mother almost
fainted when she heard the part about Father
losing the castle and everything they had,
and being hanged.

"Can I ask a question?" Father said quietly at last, and everyone turned to look at him. "Matilda, if I do fight Sir Richard and, er...lose, will your Mother still be allowed to keep Creaky Castle and all our things?"

"Of course," said Matilda with a shrug. "It's only if you refuse to accept his challenge that we would lose everything. If he beats you, then all he'll get is the cash prize for winning the tournament. He wouldn't even have to fight the other knights. But I don't think—"

"Well then," said Father. "Sir Richard, I accept your challenge!"

Chapter Nine

A Real Lifesaver

Thomas glanced at Sir Richard and saw that the knight was smiling broadly now, his mouth like a hideous gash across the bottom of his face. The crowd was yelling with excitement, and both Mother and Matilda were gabbling at the tops of their voices, begging Father not to do it.

"I'm sorry, my dears, but I've made up my mind," said Father. "I suggest we have our bout in half an hour, Sir Richard. That will give my wife time to set up a couple of other jousts to keep the crowd happy, while I get ready. Help your mother make the arrangements, Matilda. Tom, come with me."

Father turned and marched off towards the Keep, leaving Mother open-mouthed and Matilda looking very worried. Thomas hurried after him.

"I need you to give me a hand with my armour, Tom," said Father as they went inside. "We'd better send someone to get a horse saddled, too."

"Er...no problem," said Tom, and soon they were in the armoury, Thomas struggling to strap his father into a rather tight breastplate.

"Oof! I don't seem to have lost much weight on your mother's diet." Father laughed. But then he put a hand on his son's shoulder, his face suddenly serious. "Listen, Tom, if I, er...don't make it, take care of your mother and sister for me, okay? You'll be the man of the family..."

Father kept talking, but Thomas was no longer listening to him. He was far too busy thinking about the two important things he'd just realized...

The first was that he *did* have a father he could really look up to. Sir John Bailey might not be a mighty warrior like Sir Richard and the other knights, but they were horrible, and Father was good and kind, and far braver than any of them. And that was what really mattered. Father knew he couldn't beat Sir Richard, but he was willing to put his life at risk rather than let his family lose everything. Thomas thought that alone made him the best father a boy could have.

And the second thing was that he might still be able to save Father, although only if he pulled himself together – and got a move on. He still didn't know how he was going to get Sir Richard to drink the potion, but he wouldn't come up with anything if he hung around here. He needed to be out there, shadowing the Dark Knight, ready for any opportunity...

"Sorry, Father, I have to go," said Thomas, pulling the flask from his pocket and turning to leave. "I'll ask one of the men-at-arms to help you."

"Hey, what kind of soup is that?" Father said eagerly, grabbing the flask. "Thomas, you're a real lifesaver. I am absolutely *starving*..."

And before Thomas could stop him, Father uncorked the flask, lifted it to his lips, and with much glugging...drained every drop of the potion.

Thomas stood there helplessly, his own mouth open with shock. This wasn't supposed to happen. What would Faldor's potion do to Father?

"Ugh, how *disgusting*," Sir John said at last. "I don't mind cold soup if there's nothing else, but I've never tasted anything like *that* before..."

Father seemed unchanged, and for a second Thomas began to wonder if Faldor had sold him something fake. But suddenly Sir John went rigid, and his eyes bulged in their sockets. Green smoke shot out of his ears like steam from a kettle, his body started shaking, and he began to moan. The shaking and the moaning built to a peak... and stopped abruptly.

Father took a deep breath, and let it out slowly. His eyes had a faint – but definite – green tinge to them, and he had a peculiar expression on his face. It took Thomas a while to work it out, but then it hit him – Father was actually looking cross, something Thomas had never seen before.

"Er...are you okay, Father?" he asked. "I can explain, I was only–"

"*I'VE NEVER FELT BETTER IN MY LIFE, BOY!*" Father yelled, and Thomas leaped back in fright. Father made for the door, his face a mask of steely determination. "*RIGHT, SHOW TIME! I'M GOING TO MAKE THAT THUG FITZHOOLEY WISH HE'D NEVER BEEN BORN!*"

"But...but...you haven't got all your armour on yet!" stammered Thomas.

"*SO WHAT?*" roared Father as he grabbed his
sword and shield and mace and strode off.
"*I WON'T NEED THE REST, YOU STUPID
BOY! JUST BRING MY LANCE!*"

Father strode out of the armoury, swinging
his sword around as if he were already slicing
and dicing an opponent. Thomas
stayed where he was and
watched him go. This was
a very surprising turn of
events, and no mistake.

The potion seemed to have done what Faldor had claimed it would – only by a strange twist of fate, it was Father who had become the opposite of his normal self, not Sir Richard! So instead of being the least warlike knight in the kingdom, Sir John Bailey might now be the most.

Thomas felt a tiny flicker of hope. Maybe things *would* turn out for the best, and Father would survive his coming encounter with the Dark Knight. Then another thought occurred to him. What if the effect of the potion was permanent? Would Father always be like Sir Richard from now on? *And what was Mother going to say when she found out?*

Thomas groaned. It was all too difficult to think about. For a moment he found himself wishing he were asleep and having a bad dream, and that he would wake up soon. But then he heard the crowd cheering in the courtyard, and knew that it was all too real. There was nothing for it. He would have to follow this through to the end, whatever happened.

He grabbed a lance and hurried outside. A joust had just taken place, and the men-at-arms were dragging the beaten knight away by his feet. Sir John yelled at them to fetch his horse, and soon he was sitting in the saddle holding his shield, his sword and mace hanging from his belt. Thomas handed him the lance, and Father tucked it under his arm.

The crowd buzzed with interest when they saw him. But Mother gasped at the sight of her husband, and clung on to Matilda. Thomas ran to join them, passing Sir Richard, who was clanking off the other way.

"You know, I'm beginning to think this whole tournament thing might not have been quite such a good idea," said Mother. "I'll simply never be able to forgive myself if..." She paused, unable to say the words, and dabbed at her eyes. "Do you think he'll be all right, children?"

Matilda said nothing, but her grim expression was answer enough.

"Actually, I think he might..." said Thomas. He glimpsed Sparky over by the Kebab Stall. Even at such a distance he could tell that the noise of the crowd was getting to his pet dragon and making him rather skittish.

"Really?" said Mother, surprised. Matilda stared at her brother. "What makes you say that?" Mother added, her face taking on a suspicious look.

"Oh, er...well, nothing *specific*..." said Thomas, his cheeks burning.

"Oh yeah?" said Matilda. "So why did you ask me that question about the rules the other day? You know, the one about a knight at a tournament challenging the lord of the castle? I thought it was peculiar at the time..."

"*COME ON, FITZHOOLEY!*" bellowed Sir John just then, saving Thomas's bacon. "*I'M WAITING!*"

Sir Richard glowered at him, then pulled down the visor of his helmet and trotted forward to the start line at one end of the course. A deep hush fell over the crowd, and Lady Eleanor put her arms round both children, pulling them close to her. Father trotted up to his start line too, and Thomas felt his mouth go dry and his heart start hammering.

A herald stepped forward, raised his flag...then swung it down, and the two knights thundered towards each other with their lances lowered.

Thomas crossed his fingers and hoped. He could hardly bear to look...

Chapter Ten

A Total Nightmare

Sir John and the Dark Knight thundered closer
and closer together, the pounding of their horses'
hoofs echoing round the hushed courtyard.
The two knights were five lance-lengths apart,
then three, then just one, and finally they met
right on the halfway line with a terrific...*CRASH!*

And the Dark Knight was knocked head over
heels off his horse!

Thomas would never have believed it if he
hadn't seen it with his own eyes. Father's jousting

technique had been perfect. He'd hit Sir Richard in the centre of his breastplate, as if there had been a target painted on it.

The crowd couldn't quite seem to believe it either. Everybody sat still for a second, their mouths open. Then they roared their approval, Thomas punching the air and leaping up and down with his mother and sister. Only the Fitzhooley family stayed silent. Harry just looked stunned.

The Dark Knight rose unsteadily to his feet and pulled out his sword. Father dropped his lance and grabbed his mace, then wheeled his horse round and charged back the way he'd come. He thundered along...and bashed Sir Richard on the helmet with a *CLAAAAANG!* as he swept past. The Dark Knight looked surprised for an instant...then his eyes rolled up in their sockets and he fell flat on his face with a great...*CRASH!*

"*OKAY, WHO'S NEXT?*" Father roared, glaring at the other knights.

None of them seemed eager to take him on, and soon it was their turn to be jeered by the crowd. Thomas joined in, but he began to feel uneasy, especially when he realized that Mother had gone very quiet. He turned round and found her examining him with that familiar probing stare.

"I'm glad I've got your attention, Thomas," she said icily. "I've been wondering if there was anything you might want to tell me. Of course, I'm delighted your father has survived, but the more I think about it, the more I'm convinced that you've been up to something you shouldn't, especially after Matilda's little revelation. Come on, out with it..."

"I, er...don't know what you mean, Mother," whimpered Thomas. The crowd was chanting Sir John's name, the clamour growing steadily louder.

"Listen, Thomas, I wasn't born yesterday," said Mother, that stern eyebrow of hers shooting upwards. "I want the truth, and I want it *now*."

"Er...well, I..." Thomas stammered. A great roar went up as one of the other knights finally – and very reluctantly – accepted Father's challenge.

"You don't really need me here, do you, Mother?" Matilda said, giving Lady Eleanor a crafty look. "Is it okay if I go and, er...do something?"

"Yes, whatever," said Mother. Her relentless gaze

was still fixed on her son as Matilda dashed off. "I'm waiting, Thomas..." Mother said quietly.

Thomas opened his mouth to speak, but suddenly there was a loud mooing sound, and a huge burst of flame billowed briefly over the Dragon Kebab Stall. There were screams of terror, and Thomas could see a crowd of people running panic-stricken from that part of the courtyard.

"Excuse me, Mother," said Thomas. "I just want to go and check on Sparky. It looks like Mouldy might be having a, er...problem or two..."

"Hold on, Thomas, I haven't finished with you yet!" said Mother.

But Thomas was already running towards the turmoil. He had guessed that the noise of the crowd had tipped his pet dragon over the edge into hysterical excitement, and quickly discovered that he was right. Sparky had torched the Kebab Stall, and was now having fun doing the same to some of the other stalls and attractions. Mouldy was nowhere to be seen.

"Sparky, what are you *doing*?" Thomas yelled, but Sparky simply scampered away, playfully scattering more people with his swishing tail.

Thomas chased him, and Sparky eventually looked over his shoulder, purring with excitement – then fired a blast of flame at a stall stacked high with Creaky Castle souvenirs and tournament scarves, instantly burning the lot to blackened rags. Suddenly Thomas heard the sound of a horse galloping towards him, and only just got out of the way in time.

"Hey, watch yourself, little brother," yelled the rider, a knight in full armour, with lance and shield. But this was no ordinary knight, Thomas realized – it was Matilda! He watched his sister charge onto the jousting course, thunder past Father, and head straight for the knight he was about to do battle with. Matilda lowered her lance, and roared out a war cry...

After that things became, well...a little *unfocused*. It could hardly have been otherwise, what with Sparky out of control, and Father and Matilda charging around totally out of control too. They thrashed every single knight in the tournament, and declared themselves joint winners.

Thomas managed to calm his pet dragon down at last, and Matilda relaxed once she had run out of opponents. But Father just kept striding around, shouting at the servants and men-at-arms. He even aimed a kick at poor old Mott, who slunk off whining, his tail between his legs.

"Come on, Sparky," said Thomas. "I think I'd better find Mother."

Thomas would never forget the sight of Father knocking the Dark Knight off his horse – it was a memory he would always treasure. But it was beginning to look like the potion's effect *was* permanent. Thomas wanted Father restored to his old self, and he had no idea how to go about it. He hoped Mother might be able to make a suggestion, although asking her probably meant that he would finally have to confess everything.

Mother was standing by the remains of the Kebab Stall in a tragic pose, one hand over her eyes. A smiling Matilda leaned on her sword nearby.

"Er...are you okay, Mother?" said Thomas, trying to sound concerned and sympathetic. Sparky gave off one of his mournful noises.

"Let me see," Mother said, smiling weirdly at him. "The knights want their entry fees back, my daughter has behaved like a hooligan, my son's dragon has made sure we definitely *won't* make a profit, and my husband has become a monster." She paused, her smile vanishing. "In fact, today has been *a total nightmare* and I am the exact opposite of okay. The only good thing is that nobody got killed, although that might still happen..."

Mother then did a lot of shouting, but Thomas didn't listen. She had used the word *opposite*, and that had given him the answer. All they had to do was buy more of the Opposites Potion – and get Father to drink it! Another, equal dose ought to reverse the effects of the original potion.

There was a problem, though – where would they get the money to pay for it? Thomas didn't have any, and he didn't feel he could ask Mother. Suddenly, Mouldy appeared, staggering towards them with a large sack, dropping it beside Thomas. It landed with a distinct...*KER-CHINK!*

"Psst, Master Thomas!" Mouldy whispered.
"You know that little bit of change you told me to
keep...well, I thought I'd have a bet, and I put it on
Sir John. We've won loads – the odds against him
were enormous..."

Thomas looked down at the sack of money and
grinned. Suddenly, he was filled with the kind of
warm feeling you only get when everything goes

right at last. A miracle *had* happened. His problems were solved, and it was because of good old Mouldy being, well...stupidly loyal. But that, of course, was what life in Creaky Castle was all about. Sparky was purring happily, and Matilda and Mouldy were grinning now as well.

"Er...hang on a second, Mother," Thomas said, interrupting her in full flow. "Don't worry about Father. I'm sure I know how to sort him out." He did, too, and that knowledge made him feel even happier.

"Oh, is that so?" said Mother. "Well, could you sort yourself out at the same time? I'd like a lot less mischief and secrecy from you, young man!"

"I'll give it a try, Mother," said Thomas. "But nobody's perfect."

He winked at her... and ran off with Sparky to have some fun.

Everything you ever wanted to know about the author

Tony Bradman was a day-dreaming kind of child – the sort of boy who always had his nose in a book or pressed to the screen of his dirt-poor family's ancient black and white TV. So it's no surprise that he wanted to be a writer as soon as he realized that such fabulous creatures existed. Now, 200 books later, he dreams for a living, and has found himself living the dream too – with an 85-bedroom mansion in the Beverly Hills of South London, a garage full of gold-plated bikes, publishers at his beck and call, and a job where he only has to spend a couple of hours a day writing. *(He can certainly dream, can't he? – Ed.)*

Everything you ever wanted to know about the illustrator

Stephen Parkhouse wanted to draw ever since he was a toddler trying out new crayons on his bedroom wall. Mission accomplished, he now spends most of his life illustrating comic strips and graphic novels. He always liked the idea of becoming an author of children's books too, but having discovered how hugely difficult that is, he currently gets his writing fix by teaching Creative Writing at the Cumbrian Institute of the Arts.

Stephen lives in Carlisle, on the edge of Scotland and the Lake District, with assorted animals and family members.

Treachery and skulduggery, dastardly knights
and bruising battles... it's medieval mayhem
at Creaky Castle!

Tom didn't exactly get permission to buy a pet
dragon, and now that Sparky is growing so much
it's hard to keep him a secret. But could Tom's
fire-breathing friend come in handy when his family
is accused of plotting against the king?

Find out what happens in

Tom's Dragon Trouble

Out now!

ISBN 9780746072271